NOAH'S ARK

NOAH'S ARK

words from the Book of Genesis

illustrated by JANE RAY

PUFFIN BOOKS

For Clara

PUFFIN BOOKS
Published by the Penguin Group
Penguin Putnam Inc., 375 Hudson Street, New York, New York 10014, U.S.A.
Penguin Books Ltd, 27 Wrights Lane, London W8 5TZ, England
Penguin Books Australia Ltd, Ringwood, Victoria, Australia
Penguin Books Canada Ltd, 10 Alcorn Avenue, Toronto, Ontario, Canada M4V 3B2
Penguin Books (N.Z.) Ltd, 182-190 Wairau Road, Auckland 10, New Zealand

Penguin Books Ltd, Registered Offices: Harmondsworth, Middlesex, England

First published in the United States of America by Dutton Children's Books,
a division of Penguin Books USA Inc., 1990
Originally published in Great Britain by Orchard Books, The Watts Group, 1990
Published by Puffin Books, a member of Penguin Putnam Books for Young Readers, 1998

1 3 5 7 9 10 8 6 4 2

The words from the Book of Genesis have been taken from the Authorized King James Version of the Bible.

Illustrations copyright © Jane Ray, 1990
All rights reserved

THE LIBRARY OF CONGRESS HAS CATALOGED THE DUTTON EDITION AS FOLLOWS:
Bible. O.T. Genesis. English. Authorized. Selections. 1990.
Noah's ark / illustrated by Jane Ray. p. cm.
"Words from the book of Genesis."
Summary: Biblical text and illustrations depict how Noah and his family were singled out by God
to be saved from the great flood, along with two animals of each kind.
ISBN 0-525-44653-2
1. Noah's ark—Juvenile literature. [1. Noah's ark. 2. Bible O.T. Genesis.]
I Ray, Jane, ill. II. Title
BS1233.R39 1990 222'.1109505—dc20 90-32786 CIP AC

Puffin Books ISBN 0-14-056417-9

Printed in the United States of America

God saw that the wickedness of man was great
in the earth, and it grieved him at his heart.

And the Lord said, I will destroy man, and beast,
and the creeping thing, and the fowls of the air;
for it repenteth me that I have made them.

But Noah found grace in the eyes of the Lord.
Noah was a just man, and walked with God. And
Noah begat three sons, Shem, Ham, and Japheth.

And God said unto Noah, I will cause it to rain
upon the earth forty days and forty nights; and
every thing that is in the earth shall die. But with
thee will I establish my covenant.

Make thee an ark of gopher wood. Rooms shalt thou make in the ark, and shalt pitch it within and without with pitch. The length of the ark shall be three hundred cubits, the breadth of it fifty cubits, and the height of it thirty cubits.

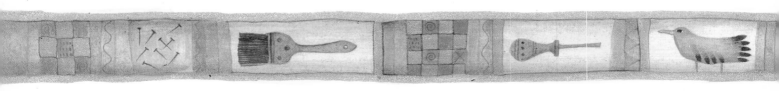

A window shalt thou make to the ark; and the
door of the ark shalt thou set in the side thereof;
with lower, second, and third stories shalt thou
make it.

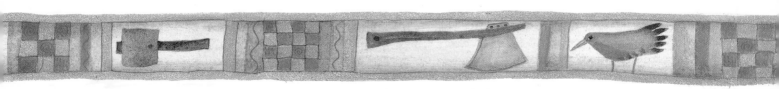

And thou shalt come into the ark, thou, and thy sons,

and thy wife, and thy sons' wives with thee.

And of every living thing of all flesh, two
of every sort shalt thou bring into the ark,

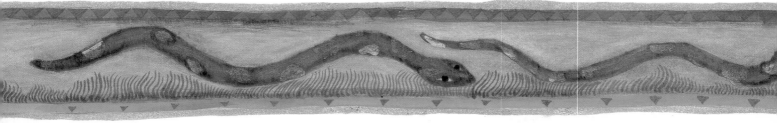

to keep them alive with thee; they shall
be male and female.

Of fowls of the air

and of beasts, and of every thing

that creepeth upon the earth.

And take thou unto thee of all food that is eaten; and it shall be for food for thee, and for them. Thus did Noah, according to all that God commanded him.

And it came to pass after seven days, that the waters of the flood were upon the earth. The windows of heaven were opened; and the ark went upon the face of the waters.

And all the high hills, that were
under the whole heaven, were covered.

And the mountains were covered.

Every living substance was destroyed which was
upon the ground, both man, and cattle, and the
creeping things, and the fowl of the heaven; and

Noah only remained alive, and they that were
with him in the ark.

And God remembered Noah, and made a wind
to pass over the earth. The rain from heaven
was restrained, and the ark rested upon the
mountains of Ararat. And the waters decreased
continually until the tops of the mountains were
seen.

And at the end of forty days Noah opened
the window of the ark and sent forth a dove,

to see if the waters were abated from off the ground. But she found no rest for the sole of her foot and returned into the ark.

And again Noah sent forth the dove; and the dove came in to him in the evening; and in her mouth was an olive leaf: so Noah knew that the waters were abated from off the earth. And at the end of seven days Noah again sent forth the dove, which returned not unto him any more.

And Noah removed the covering of the ark, and looked, and, behold, the face of the ground was dry. And God spake unto Noah, saying, I will set my bow in the cloud, and it shall be a token of a covenant between me and you and every living creature.

Go forth of the ark, thou, and thy wife, and thy
sons, and thy sons' wives with thee. Bring forth
with thee every living thing that is with thee, both
of fowl, and of cattle, and of every creeping thing

that creepeth upon the earth. Be fruitful, and
multiply, and replenish the earth, for I will not
curse the ground any more.

And while the earth remaineth, seedtime and harvest, and cold and heat, and summer and winter, and day and night shall not cease.